THANK YOU
FOR LOOKING
AFTER OUR PETS

For Gillian & Pen

SIMON AND SCHUSTER
First published in Great Britain in 2011
by Simon and Schuster UK Ltd
1st Floor, 222 Gray's Inn Road, London, WC1X 8HB
A CBS Company

A CIP catalogue record for this book is available
from the British Library upon request

978 0 85707 114 9 (HB)
978 0 85707 115 6 (PB)
Printed in China
10 9 8 7 6 5 4 3 2 1

THANK YOU FOR LOOKING AFTER OUR PETS

Tim Hopgood

SIMON AND SCHUSTER
London   New York   Sydney

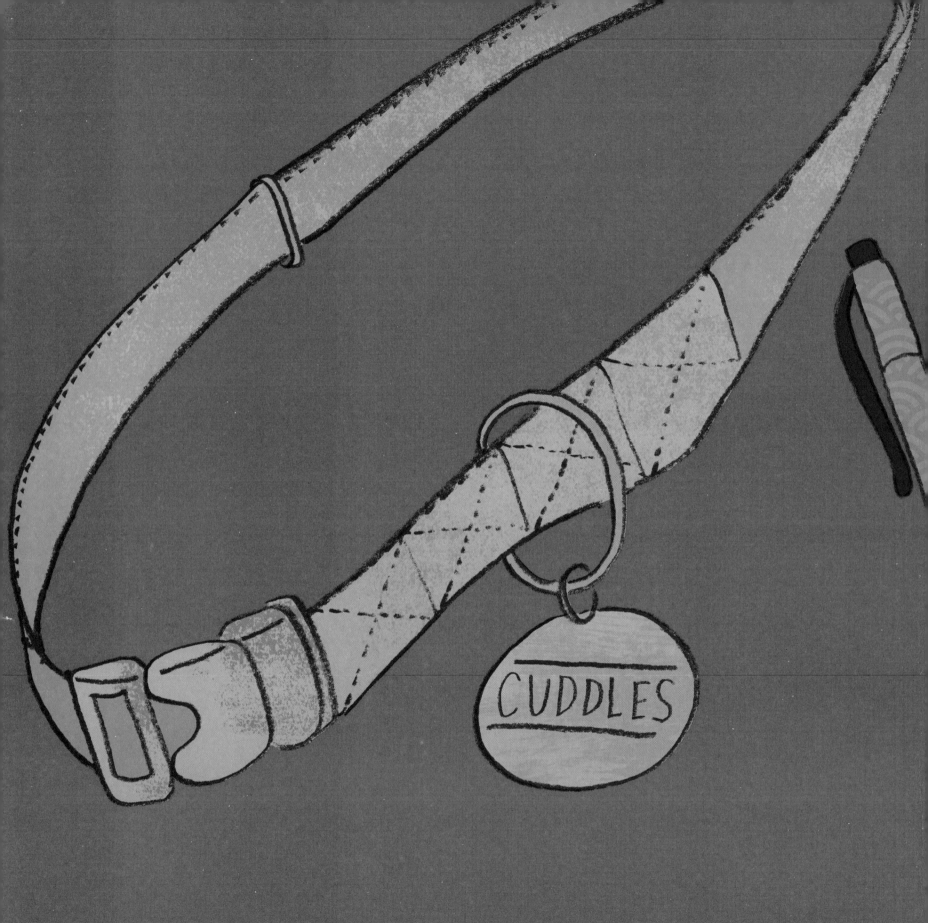

It's very kind of you to look after

our pets while we're away.

I've written a few notes for you.

There's quite a lot to remember.

First of all there's Cuddles . . .

It's probably best if she has breakfast first.
She's always hungry in the morning and
can get a little grumpy.

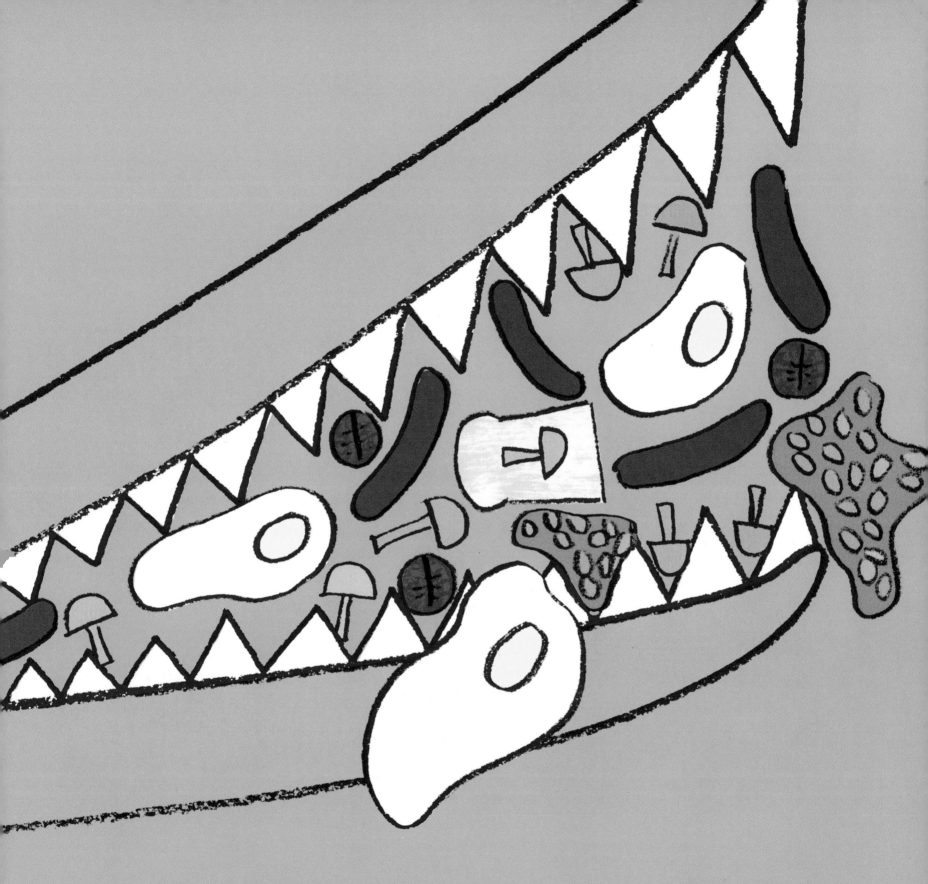

Don't forget to brush her teeth afterwards!

Don't worry about Spock.
He likes a long sleep,
so he'll have his breakfast
later.

If he starts shedding,
please can you put his
old skin in the bin.

Watch out for Ping and Pong.

They like to dance on the stairs.

But don't let them make too much noise because
Elsie and Edna like a mid-morning snooze.

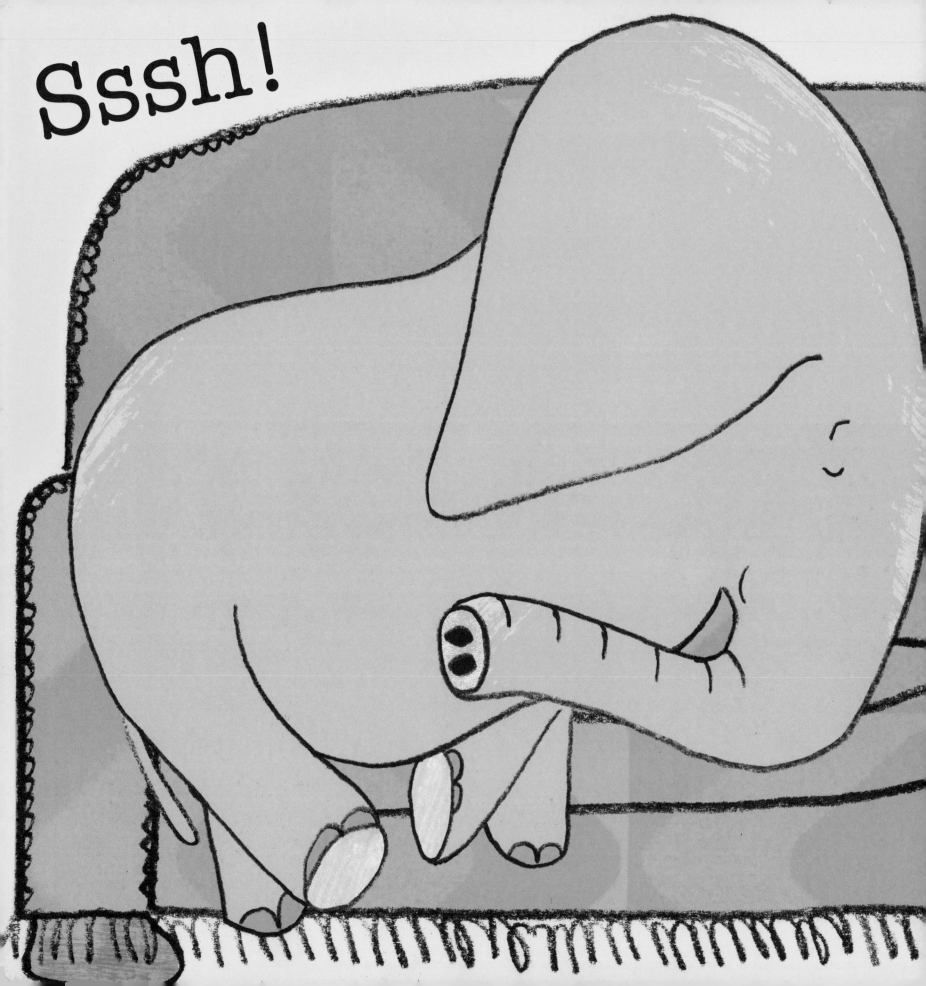

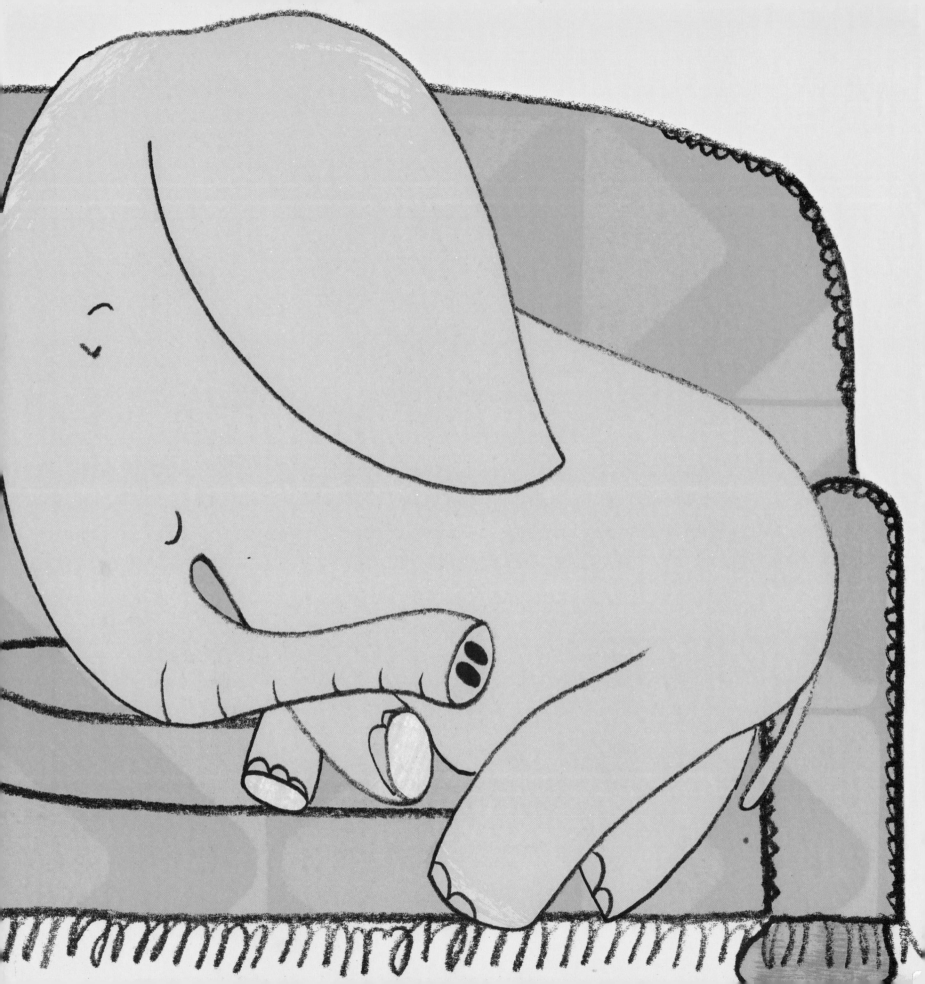

Please clean out Vincent's cage at least once a day.

Don't worry, he doesn't bite!

After lunch, George and Ringo like a stroll in the park.

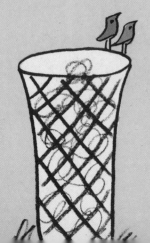

But whatever you do,
don't forget the poopa-scoopa.

You'll need it!

Tea-time can be a bit messy.

Keep your eye on Burt
or he'll try to eat the lot!

Winston enjoys being tickled,
especially on his tummy.

But you'll have to catch him first!

Orlando likes a bath before bedtime.

Don't forget the bubbles.
Orlando loves bubbles!

And finally, remember to put
the cat out last thing at night . . .

ROAR!

Oh, and just one more thing.
If you get the chance, would you mind
watering the plants?

But do take care . . .

... they bite!

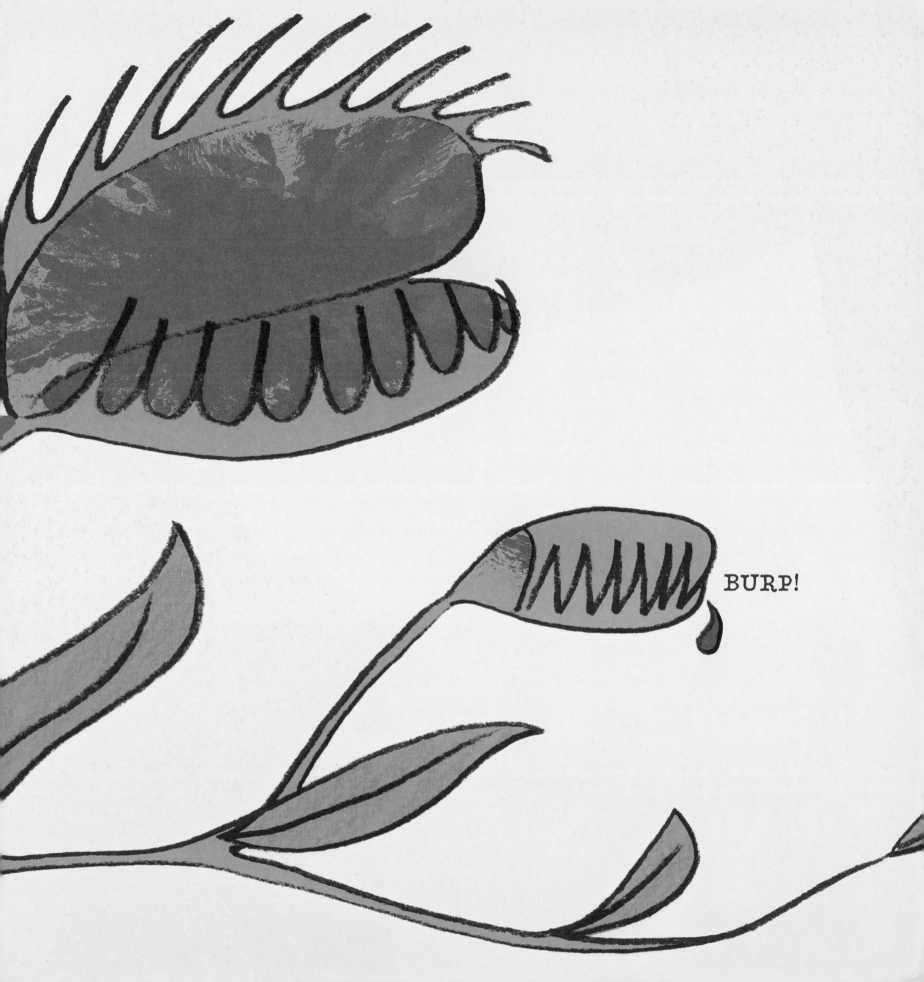

We'll be back next Saturday
(all being well).

THANK YOU
x

Any problems, our number
is on the fridge.